MY FIRST STORY 2016

Welcome!

Dear Reader,

Welcome to a world of imagination!

My First Story was designed for 5-7 year-olds as an introduction to creative writing and to promote an enjoyment of reading and writing from an early age.

The simple, fun storyboards give even the youngest and most reluctant writers the chance to become interested in literacy by giving them a framework within which to shape their ideas. Pupils could also choose to write without the storyboards, allowing older children to let their creativity flow as much as possible, encouraging the use of imagination and descriptive language.

We believe that seeing their work in print will inspire a love of reading and writing and give these young writers the confidence to develop their skills in the future.

There is nothing like the imagination of children, and this is reflected in the creativity and individuality of the stories in this anthology. I hope you'll enjoy reading their first stories as much as we have.

Jenni Bannister

Editorial Manager

Ima ine. .

Each child was given the beginning of a story and then chose one of five storyboards, using the pictures and their imagination to complete the tale. You can view the storyboards at the end of this book.

The Beginning...

One night Ellie was woken by a tapping at her window.

It was Spencer the elf! 'Would you like to go on an adventure?' he asked.

They flew above the rooftops. Soon they had arrived...

South London Adventures

Contents

Amelia Ashpitel (6)	68
Elijah Quartey (6)	69
Callum Campbell-Mackay (6)	70
Sofia Rosa Robinson (6)	71
Elisabeth Zemskov (6)	72
Ashton Savva Burrowes (5)	73
Abdullah Rayyan (6)	74

Thomas's Academy, London

Jack Hugo de Piro O'Connell (7)	75
Ghaliyah Esmail (7)	76
Oscyra Moses (7)	78
Channai Chambers (7)	79
Malakai Maxwell-Roberts (7)	80
Natalja Gilles (7)	81
Zaynab Abouchouche (7)	82
Elias Oualah (7)	83
Alex Edward Thorne (7)	84
Inas Khelfaoui (7)	85
Amir Mohamoud (7)	86

Trinity St Mary's CE Primary School, London

Adomas Mucinskas (7)	87
Renan Carias (7)	88
Zahra Fatema Khimani (7)	89
Elijah Marley Walker (7)	90
Dougal Hamilton (7)	91
David Oyat Loum (7)	92
Hirad Baghi (7)	93
Natalia Paluch (7)	94
Christian Jermaine Pottinger (7)	95
Brooke Humphreys (7)	96
Elioenai Gordon (6)	97
Ratib Mulindwa Kalikka (6)	98
Eden Shalom (7)	99
Noah Destalem (7)	100
Alexander Kolbuc (7)	101
Mikayla Hornsby-Odoi	102

Westminster Cathedral RC Primary School, London

Franek Wielogorski (7)	103
Mateusz Krol (6)	104
Ruby-Belle Sweeney (7)	105
Alexandra Maria Taylor (6)	106
Lisa Leese (7)	107
Daniella Ortiz Posso (7)	108
Bobby Barnes (6)	110
Marvel Yao Ashvin Sebastien N'zi (7)	111
Julia Maire Dela Cuesta (7)	112
Jessica Rebelo (7)	114
Daisy Riley (7)	115
Amy Leigh Dunn (7)	116
Dylan Gething (6)	117
Harry Antony Hurley (7)	118
Akua Oppong (7)	119
Aaron Jeriah Barclay (7)	120
Isabella De Freitas (7)	121
Daniel Germachew Mulugeta (7)	122
Frederick Oloke (7)	123
Logan Watts (7)	124
Tia Williams (6)	125
Eva Ornelas (6)	126
Bettiel Tech-Lu (6)	127
Samuel Emanuel (6)	128
Santiago Silva Pereira (6)	129
Edward Chahin (6)	130
Connie Collins-Platt (6)	131
Iara Machado Costa (6)	132
Sophia Soares (6)	133
Samira Chaud (7)	134

The Stories

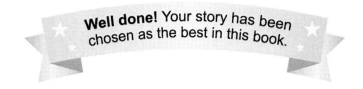

Well done! Your story has been chosen as the best in this book.

Nina's Magical Story

Ellie and Spencer met a kind unicorn named Katie. All of them flew to Unicorn World.

The unicorn told Ellie and Spencer the story of the scary dragon who haunted little unicorns, the dragon had really sharp claws and long teeth and breathed fire.

Ellie, Spencer and the bear were so scared that they ran away.

They found Katie and they hopped on her back and flew to find a witch for help. After a while they found a witch. Witch Angela said, 'The only way to stop a dragon is to find a magic key on a clifftop and find a way to make the dragon choke on it.'

Ellie and Spencer flew on the broom and found the key in a small house. There they worked on their plan...

They came back to Unicorn World to find the dragon. Ellie and her friends tickled the dragon and the dragon opened his mouth and laughed then Spencer threw the key in the dragon's mouth.

1

Then the dragon turned into a kind and lovely baby dragon. From now on the dragon and all of the unicorns were friends.
Finally Ellie was home and slept after the whole adventure.

Nina Rzoska (7)
All Saints' CE Primary School, London

Leiah's Jungle Story

Spencer and Ellie arrived at a jungle, a green, browny jungle. They swung over the pond, around a tree and over a monkey until they got to the most mysterious thing in the jungle.

It was... a snake! The snake was green and blue, orange and yellow, it was a mysterious snake. The snake was swirly, whirly and twirly. The children looked very scared, they walked away very slowly. Suddenly, the snake turned around. 'It looks very scary!' said Ellie. They ran and ran and ran as fast as they could. They got into the middle of the jungle.

They stopped very scared because they were about to bump into a lion. 'Argh!'

'Have you seen a lion before?' the lion said. 'Hop on my back, I won't hurt you.' So they hopped on. The lion gave them a tour all around the jungle until the end of the jungle. That was how caring the lion was. The lion said it was late and it was time to go home.

They went over the pond, around the trees and over a monkey's head. They all started to yawn. They were finally home sweet home.

Leiah Ivel Lobban (7)
All Saints' CE Primary School, London

3

Deborah's Magical Story

When Ellie and Ben arrived they saw some magical unicorns, they were having a party.

Everything went quiet. Suddenly, behind them were big, prickly, pointy and sharp claws, it was a dragon!

Emily said to Ben, 'Run!' The dragon gave Ben and Emily a chance. It kept breathing fire, burning everything on the way. Emily and Ben ran like a cheetah for their dear lives. They came upon a huge valley with the dragon at their tail with the eyes as red as burning coal.

As they stood at edge of the valley ready to be devoured by the dragon, there appeared a tiny teddy bear. It shouted, 'Close your eyes and jump.' Ben and Emily closed their eyes and did exactly that, knowing that they were jumping to their death. However, they landed comfortably on the back of a unicorn instead of the valley with the dragon inches away. Emily sighed, 'Phew! We were a whisker away from death.'

The unicorn then flew them to a witch's house. On the way they entered through a hole as small as an ant hole. After that they entered into an ocean, then they came upon a large golden entrance. It opened by itself.

They entered a city. Everything in the city is made of gold. The unicorn then took them to a witch. The witch had a croaky voice and her nails were as long as Mount Everest.

Emily and Ben said to the witch, 'We are hungry, can we get something to eat?'

The witch said, 'Go outside and pick some stones, put them in a bowl and put it on the fire.'

Ben said, 'Excuse me?'

But Emily said, 'Do as she said.' Ben put the stones on fire and it turned into a delicious meal.

Emily and Ben wanted to know how to get home so they asked the witch and she gave them a broom to sit on. The witch lifted up her long hands and the broom also lifted up and flew like rocket. In no time they were flying above their town with no one noticing and landed in their garden.

Emily's mother was just coming into the garden. She asked Emily, 'Where have you been? I have been calling you to come and do your homework.'

Ben opened his mouth and said, 'We just landed from a...'

But then Emily interrupted and said, 'We just landed from a friend's house.' Of course Emily knew she was not making sense but she was doing everything to hide the truth of their adventure.

But Emily mother said, 'Landed from a friend's house? That does not make any sense to me. Now go and do your homework and say bye-bye to Ben,' shouted Emily's mother.

Deborah Diawuo (7)
All Saints' CE Primary School, London

Maria's Pirate Story

Once upon a time a little girl called Ellie found a nice elf. They were finding a treasure to make a house with some toys for children to share with and live.

They arrived on the island with a box full of shiny coins and pearls.

Soon a nasty pirate had arrived. He had a sharp sword and he wanted to take the treasure from them.

The nasty pirate made them walk the plank but the elf had magic powers so the elf made a trick.

He made a plastic box with plastic coins in it. He left the plastic treasure in the ship and made the real treasure invisible so they could take it home.

The pirate took the plastic treasure and the children took the real treasure. Two nice dolphins then came and took them to land.

Ellie and the elf then went home happily. They couldn't wait for their next adventure.

Maria Sier Martinon (6)

All Saints' CE Primary School, London

Rhianna's Magical Story

Alexandra the unicorn was very special. Alexandra could go underwater, she would blow a big bubble from her horn.

Ellie and Spencer went underwater. Suddenly, a water dragon appeared out of nowhere and said, 'Who are you and what do you want?'

Ellie and Spencer said they wanted to see Princess Pearl, the mermaid, for the magical ring of hearts to take them home. The water dragon laughed and said, 'I am going to eat you up.'

Ellie and Spencer were scared. The water dragon started to chase them. Luckily, Alexandra used her magical powers and they floated away as fast as they could.

Spencer was very hungry as they rode safely to land so they stopped to look for food. Out of nowhere appeared an ugly, crooked old witch. The witch said she had food in her house.

Ellie and Spencer went to her house, it was made of candy. They started to eat so much candy they fell asleep.

When they woke up they found the magical ring of hearts under the old witch's crooked broomstick.

Once they touched the ring the magic started to begin. They sat on the witch's broom and off they went. They stopped by the sea and saw Pearl and gave her the ring back. Pearl made a wish and off they went home.

Rhianna Rahman (7)
All Saints' CE Primary School, London

Aleeza's Magical Story

Ellie was taken on a beautiful unicorn. Spencer the elf wanted to show Ellie where he came from: Rainbow Land.

In this land lived a dragon. Spencer the elf told Ellie it was Rowan the dragon, Rowan was a lovely, friendly dragon but today Rowan had a cough and every time he coughed he breathed fire.

Ellie screamed, 'I don't like this.'

'Nor do I,' said Spencer. Rowan was out of control. 'Let's go get help!'

Ellie and Spencer jumped on the beautiful unicorn and went to find the wise old witch for help.

They explained to the witch the problem with Rowan so she gave them a potion for him.

The potion worked perfectly and Rowan was better. Spencer said, 'Ellie, you have to now go home.'

Aleeza Miah (6)
All Saints' CE Primary School, London

Ella's Jungle Story

Spencer and Ellie found themselves in a wet and damp jungle. They swung from tree to tree using strong green vines.

Ellie and Spencer met a mischievous snake in the wet and damp jungle. The snake said, 'I am going to eat you!'

They quickly ran away in the wet and damp jungle. They met a furry lion. The lion said, 'Would you like to come on a tour of the jungle?'

'Yes please,' they said.

They did, they went all around the wet and damp jungle.

It was time to go home so Ellie and Spencer grabbed a vine each and swung home.

Ella Kirk (7)

All Saints' CE Primary School, London

Oscar's Magical Story

Ellie and the handsome elf went on a beautiful unicorn. That wasn't too bad!
They met a fierce dragon that breathed fire. How big is that dragon?
The evil dragon started roaring and chased them!
Suddenly, they saw the unicorn and went on the beautiful unicorn.
Then a witch came and said, 'Are you in trouble?'
'Yes,' said the girl.
They then hopped on the broom and went home where they lived happily ever after.

Oscar Ford (7)
All Saints' CE Primary School, London

Jenae's Jungle Story

Ellie and Spencer the elf swung onto the trees and they also climbed with David the mischievous bear. All three of them swung really fast.

On their way to the jungle they saw the hissing snake, which was trying to catch Ellie and Spencer but the snake couldn't because Spencer and Ellie were very clever because they remembered to wear their fast running shoes.

Five minutes later the snake attempted to scare Spencer and Ellie, but then they ran away from the hissing snake and they never saw the hissing snake again.

A few minutes later when they lost sight of the hissing snake they saw a lion. The lion asked them if they wanted a ride on his back and they all jumped on his back with excitement because they were being rescued from the hissing snake.

After the ride on the racing lion's back they got a bit tired and wanted to go back home.

They swung back home on the prickly trees. Ellie said, 'What a lovely adventure meeting a lion and a hissing snake,' and the lion never saw them again.

Jenae Henry (7)
All Saints' CE Primary School, London

William's Space Story

...at a planet far, far away. Flying through the sky and up into space was exciting. I held tightly onto Spencer as we were flying very fast and we had arrived in no time.

The planet had craters the size of dumper truck tyres and we could easily touch the bright shining stars up in the sky. A green smiling alien came over and said, 'Hello, my name is Graham.' He asked if we would like a ride in his spaceship. Before we could answer he had vanished but quickly returned with what looked like a huge upside-down saucer with a glass bubble on top.

He beamed us up into the spaceship and we were off! The ride was smooth and lots of fun. Graham's friend joined us in another saucer-shaped ship and together we went to another planet. This was large, round and very bright. Our ship glided towards the surface and in front of us there was an orange creature with three eyes, a long tongue and tentacles. We took lots of photos but it was getting late and we had to leave. Graham said he could take us back home. As quick as a flash we had arrived back home.

I said to Spencer, 'Thank you for a great time together,' and waved goodbye as Graham flew up into the sky and out of sight.

William Elgar (6)
All Saints' CE Primary School, London

Thaanya's Jungle Story

Spencer and Ellie jumped from building to building and, at last, reached the jungle. They swung to another branch and Ellie said, 'It's funny.' They met a small teddy bear and played until they got tired. They saw a large red snake on a branch of a big tree. The snake scared the children and they ran and hid under branches.

It made the children very scared so they walked away.

They hid behind the bush and heard a snoring sound. It was a lion. He woke up with a smiling face. He heard their story and offered to help. Lion Simba was very friendly.

Lion Simba carried Ellie, Spencer and Teddy Bear behind his back, all three enjoyed their ride. The lion safely took them towards the end of the jungle and asked Ellie to visit him again.

Ellie and Spencer gave Teddy Bear a big hug. At last Ellie and Spencer flew back to Ellie's house. Ellie enjoyed her adventure and went back to sleep.

Thaanya Sivakaran (7)
All Saints' CE Primary School, London

Nyah's Pirate Story

'Let's go to the beach,' said Ellie and they rowed the boat to shore. They saw an island and rowed there to get to their destination.

When Ellie and Spencer got there they started looking for an old treasure chest, it had gold and silver with jewels and money inside.

A pirate got the treasure and hid the treasure on his ship.

The pirate commanded Ellie and Spencer to walk the plank. Spencer went first, Ellie was scared. In the corner was a dolphin and Spencer said it would just watch.

Spencer was wrong, the dolphin saved them and jumped in the air. It was getting dark so they went home to get Ellie to bed.

Spencer got Ellie home so her mummy didn't know and the same with Spencer. Spencer had got the pirate hat and Ellie had one too. 'Night-night,' she said.

Nyah Joanna Salako (7)
All Saints' CE Primary School, London

Perpetua's Magical Story

The unicorn took Ellie and Spencer to a dragon's house. Do you think they are going to enjoy the whole ride?

The dragon scared Ellie and Spencer and they thought the dragon was going to kill them with the poisonous scales. 'I'm scared!' cried Ellie and Spencer.

Ellie and Spencer ran away from the dragon. The dragon really wanted to kill them because he was getting his fire ready.

Afterwards they found the unicorn and the unicorn took them to a witch's home. Ellie and Spencer didn't know where the unicorn was taking them, only the unicorn knew.

The witch tried to kill them like the dragon did. She was going to use her sharp nails to kill them.

Finally, they found a broom and flew back home. If you had a trip like that would you like it?

Perpetua Dokua Acheampong (7)
All Saints' CE Primary School, London

Shania's Zoo Story

Ellie and the Elf appeared at Battersea Park Zoo and said hello to a cute elephant. They called her Nellie.

They decided to take a tour of the zoo on Nellie, along with her cuddly bear. They enjoyed watching all the animals jumping, singing and dancing around the zoo.

They visited a big black and white panda bear with his puppy. They called him Andy Pandy.

They continued their tour of the zoo, on good old Nellie and her pet. They seemed to be having an excellent time.

Later they met Mr Gorilla called George and stopped for a snack of bananas. The bananas were delicious.

After a long adventure visiting friends at the zoo, Elf said goodbye to Ellie and returned home on Nellie. 'Goodbye everybody, didn't we have a great day?'

Shania Douglas (6)

All Saints' CE Primary School, London

A Magic Adventure

In a mythical land where myths began a unicorn wanted to give the girl Ellie and Spencer the elf a ride so they hopped on and off they went.

All of a sudden an evil dragon made them fall off because he wanted them in his belly as he was hungry.

They ran as fast as they could. They did not stop. They didn't give up. They kept on going.

Soon they found the unicorn again. They hopped on and got away from the nasty dragon.

Soon they met a witch who said, 'Do you want some candy?' The unicorn was scared and made them fall off. They quickly ran away in fear.

They found the witch's magic broom and flew all the way home. Ellie then went back to bed and fell asleep. And Spencer, he went home and cooked some food.

Elizabeth Avedisyan (7)
All Saints' CE Primary School, London

Jedaiah's Magical Story

Once upon a time there lived an elf called Spencer, he wanted to go on an adventure with Ellie, a little girl. The elf's unicorn was flying gracefully. They passed many countries like Saudi Arabia and continents like Europe. The ride was long.
When they got to a land of princes and princess they had to get past a mighty, massive dragon. They couldn't, the dragon just scared them away like they were tiny ants. They were so frightened that they fell over.
The unicorn took the little girl back to get some sleep.
When they were about halfway through, they met an ugly witch, but she was nice and gentle.
The kind witch lent them her broom. Spencer gave his unicorn to the witch and the girl got some sleep.

Jedaiah Bannerman (7)
All Saints' CE Primary School, London

Maryam's Space Story

Ellie and Spencer the elf arrived in space. They flew to another planet.

They arrived at the moon and saw an alien. They ran on the moon, then the alien appeared. 'Do not worry, I am not going to hurt you, I am a friendly alien.'

Then the alien beamed them up in the spaceship and it sucked up Ellie, Teddy and also Spencer the elf.

They met another spaceship and said hello. 'Hello,' the other spaceship said.

They were attacked by a horrible monster. They put down a ladder to the other spaceship and climbed down the ladder to the other spaceship. The alien then flew back to Earth and Ellie went back home and said goodbye.

Maryam Malik (6)

All Saints' CE Primary School, London

Max's Space Story

In space Ellie and Spencer were heading to the moon. Ellie was so amazed that she went crazy and was going all over the place.

When they reached the moon they came across an alien and it was friendly. When they saw it, Ellie was terrified but the alien was trying to make her happy.

The alien wanted Ellie to have a trip so he sucked her into his spaceship.

After that the alien showed them around space to see how cool it was and then they saw a monster! First they looked at the greedy monster, it wanted to eat them but it didn't eat them because they zoomed off.

Finally, Ellie went back to Earth, went home and went to bed.

Max Lushi (7)
All Saints' CE Primary School, London

Aisha's Pirate Story

Ellie and Spencer flew until they saw a small boat. They sailed for five days eating sushi on the way. On the sixth day they found an island that had some treasure on it. Spencer said, 'We should be careful because it might belong to a pirate.' Suddenly, a rude pirate shouted, 'Get away from my glorious treasure right now!' He really scared Ellie and Spencer.

The mean pirate made them walk the plank even though they were trying to explain that they didn't want the treasure.

Luckily some kind dolphins gave them a ride to their comfy homes.

They were both home before the sun came up!

Aisha Monique Frater (7)

All Saints' CE Primary School, London

Roman's Jungle Story

Ellie and Spencer were swinging on a vine that was hanging from the green tree, it was exciting!
There was a green snake trying to get them. The children felt scared as the snake was hissing.
The snake was trying to catch the children. They ran as fast as a cheetah.
The lion came and it was a friendly lion. The lion said, 'You can get on my back.'
The lion was trying to run away from the snake. The snake was so tired and the snake gave up.
At the end of the day they were swinging on the vine again. Finally, they saw their house and they lived happily in their house.

Roman Agha (6)
All Saints' CE Primary School, London

Chaii's Magical Story

My dragon, Mrs Unicorn, a wizard called Tizar and I are in a fascinating place that has huge amounts of animals.

We see dragons who are huge and run away. The unicorns are there. They look scary but we ride them. If you ever get a chance to ride one please do!

Now we have to make our way home so we jump back onto the unicorn and leave the world of the unknown.

However, the adventure has only just begun!

On the way home we see a witch. The witch offers her broomstick to us.

We travel back home. It is a long night so we tuck ourselves into bed and go to sleep.

Chaii Carty (7)

All Saints' CE Primary School, London

Ioana's Pirate Story

Ellie and Spencer were going on a long canoe!
They wanted to find out if they could find anything.
Finally, they found money and gold. Ellie didn't see
a pirate ship but Spencer saw that and a kind
teddy bear came.

A pirate came with a parrot and took their money
and took them to his pirate ship.

Soon the pirate made them go into the water. The
first one was Spencer, then Ellie.

The dolphins helped. They knew that from the
teddy bear! What a brave teddy bear!

They were home with the helpful, kind, fun teddy
bear and they finally were happy forever.

Ioana Baluta (7)
All Saints' CE Primary School, London

Charlie's Magical Story

At Unicorn World Ellie and Spencer went looking for unicorn treasure. One unicorn had got a sharp point at the end of its horn.

A dragon appeared out of the blue and frightened Ellie and Spencer. They ran away quickly.

The dragon chased Ellie, Teddy and Spencer but they could run very, very fast and got away.

Suddenly, they saw a tail and it was a unicorn and it flew all the way home to rest.

They saw a witch so Ellie went into the witch's house and got the broomstick and flew home. When they got home they went to bed straight away.

Charlie Broughton (6)

All Saints' CE Primary School, London

Milko's Magical Story

Ellie and Spencer travelled to the top of a hill on the back of an adult unicorn.

A dragon had found Ellie and Spencer. The dragon started to breathe burning fire.

Ellie and Spencer ran away from their fire-breathing dragon. The dragon didn't know they had run away.

Ellie and Spencer then went back onto the unicorn and they went to a witch's house.

A witch had found Ellie and Spencer. The witch let them have her broom.

Ellie and Spencer flew back home. They had a good day.

Milko Lewis (7)

All Saints' CE Primary School, London

Asvinth's Magical Story

Ellie and Spencer arrived at the tropical and exotic island called Sun Island. It was amazing!
While they were exploring they met an evil fire-breathing dragon. They started to run.
They ran across the soft, comfortable sand with their friend, Teddy.
They found a unicorn called Slimy and he took them to Chocolate Island and found a toffee house.
They met a witch who looked evil but she was good. They were stunned.
She gave them a broomstick and they flew happily away.

Asvinth Sooriyapalan (6)
All Saints' CE Primary School, London

Mathushan's Pirate Story

As Jack spotted an island he went there because he was hungry.

As Jack went on the island he saw a treasure box, it was full of gold. Then he saw a bad pirate.

As the pirates came they were very cross because they had touched their treasure.

As Jack and Milly touched the treasure chest the pirates punished them and made them walk the plank.

As they walked the plank they saw dolphins and jumped on them.

As they jumped on the dolphins the dolphins dropped them off.

Mathushan Sivanenthiran (5)

All Saints' CE Primary School, London

Oliwia's Zoo Story

Ellie and Spencer went off to explore the zoo with lots of animals.

First they went to the elephants and rode them and it looked like fun. They were smiling at each other while riding.

Next they went to the pandas with fluffy white and black fur.

They then went back on the elephant to the next stop.

They stopped at the gorillas and monkeys and they were really cheeky and holding bananas in their hands.

Finally they went back on the elephant who took Ellie home.

Oliwia Kruglik (6)

All Saints' CE Primary School, London

Thenuja's Magical Story

Ellie and Spencer the elf went on a pink, sparkling unicorn through a castle.

Ellie suddenly saw an angry, enormous dragon with sharp white teeth. She was scared.

Ellie and Spencer ran as fast as they could as the dragon chased them.

They jumped on the unicorn and as it ran fast. They were safe at last.

After that they saw a witch, Ellie and Spencer were scared.

Ellie wasn't scared now because the witch got them a magical broom so they flew home.

Thenuja Jeyakaran (5)
All Saints' CE Primary School, London

Dheer's Space Story

On the moon the boy and girl were going to the sparkly stars.

When they got there they were collecting stars, there was a cheeky alien, it wasn't going to hurt them, it was going to give them a ride.

The girl was having a ride with the cheeky alien. She was soon saying goodbye when she heard an ugly burp.

It was a horrible monster, it wanted to eat the spaceship and they escaped.

They were going home, the flying elf was gong home too.

Dheer Bhatt (7)

All Saints' CE Primary School, London

Jensen's Space Story

Ellie and Spencer arrived in space, it was full of stars. It was called Alien Land.

The alien was called Dave and he was sad and cross.

Dave took Ellie in his flying saucer to show her how clean and wonderful space was.

Ellie was trying to touch the stars but she couldn't.

They met a funny monster with three eyes and a long tongue.

Ellie promised to tell everyone to respect the Earth and said goodbye to Dave and Spencer.

Jensen Armir Jacques Peposhi (6)

All Saints' CE Primary School, London

Dexter's Space Story

Spencer and Ellie went to Planet Cake. Ellie was amazed, the whole planet was a big cake!
Ellie was hungry so she started to eat it.
An alien appeared and sucked her and her teddy up.
He took them for a ride.
Next, on one of the planets was a monster called Gobster, he tried to eat them! He got out his sticky tongue to lick her up!
However, he missed and the alien took Ellie safely back home.

Dexter Dawson (7)
All Saints' CE Primary School, London

Rowan's Space Story

Ellie and Spencer flew into space and were hovering above the Earth and under the stars. They landed on the moon and the elf caught two stars and they saw an alien!
The alien picked up Ellie and flew into the stars.
The other spaceship behind shone its light.
Suddenly, a monster appeared and they picked it up just before it ate them.
They flew back to Earth and dropped Ellie off.

Rowan Sedgwick (6)
All Saints' CE Primary School, London

Jayden's Pirate Story

First, Spencer and Ellie were on a boat on an adventure to find treasure.
They found treasure and so much gold and a crown!
When they found a treasure chest, a pirate came.
The pirate let them get on his ship.
Next, both of them were riding dolphins.
Finally, they were all tired and it was night-time.
They walked home.

Jayden Lee (7)
All Saints' CE Primary School, London

Sonny's Magical Story

One day Spencer and Ellie were going on an adventure and they arrived at a magic land.
In the middle of the adventure they saw a big dragon.
They ran away from the dragon.
They went back home on a unicorn.
On the way back they saw an ugly woman.
They were soon home.

Sonny Byrne (5)
All Saints' CE Primary School, London

Leo's Pirate Story

Spencer and Ellie are rowing the boat together.
They find gold and the boy looks unhappy.
They find a pirate called Brownbeard.
The boy walks the plank and the girl looks sad.
They're riding dolphins and having fun.
They are walking home.

Leo-Justin Hassan (6)
All Saints' CE Primary School, London

Sina's Pirate Story

Ellie and her friend went for an adventure and they got in a boat.
When they got to the island they found treasure.
A pirate then came for his treasure.
After that they walked the plank.
Some dolphins were there.
Then they walked home.

Sina Navabi (7)
All Saints' CE Primary School, London

Michael's Pirate Story

Ellie and Spencer landed on a boat on an island.
They found treasure!
Suddenly the pirates came!
They made Spencer walk the plank but...
The dolphins were catching them!
They went home and lived happily ever after.

Michael Dmochowski (6)
All Saints' CE Primary School, London

Dhru's Magical Story

Ellie and Spencer went to a sparkly pony named Stardust. 'Would you like a ride on me?' she said. They went off until they lost the pony!

Soon a dragon found them and wanted to have them for dinner! Spencer the elf had a plan. He got taken. Suddenly, he bit the dragon's finger!

They ran and ran. The dragon tried to breathe fire to burn them for dinner until they lost him.

Afterwards, Spencer and Ellie found a unicorn and had a ride to Candy Land, it was fun grabbing sweets.

Soon they found a wicked witch, she wanted to put a spell on them. They finally had another plan so Spencer picked up Ellie and took the witch's broom! They flew across Candy Land and the forests to Ellie's garden. Finally they were home!

Dhru Sai Bhatia (6)
All Saints' CE Primary School, London

Finley's Jungle Story

Spencer the elf tapped on Ellie's window and said, 'Do you want to come on an adventure?'

Ellie said, 'Yes,' and took her teddy with her.

Soon they all lived in the jungle together. They met a snake but he was not friendly and said, 'I'm going to eat you.'

The snake was so slow and fat he could not keep up. Spencer, Teddy and Ellie ran so fast the snake couldn't even catch them.

Next a friendly lion said, 'Do you want a lift?'

They said, 'Yes.'

'Where do you want to go?'

'To the end of the jungle please!'

The lion picked them up and left them all at the end of the jungle and said goodbye.

Spencer, Teddy and Ellie swung through vines and got back home safely.

Finley Michalak (6)
Archbishop Sumners Primary School, London

Zoë's Magical Story

Ellie and Spencer had arrived at a magical forest. Suddenly, Spencer saw an amazing unicorn. They jumped on. They told the unicorn to go somewhere where they could have an adventure and the unicorn did.

Suddenly, a dragon appeared. It was so scary and it even could breathe green fire! Ellie and Spencer were so scared. Even Ellie's teddy was scared.

They ran away as fast as possible. Ellie tried to find the unicorn. Then it suddenly appeared.

They jumped on it again. Ellie, Spencer and the unicorn travelled to every land and when they were about to leave the magical forest the unicorn bumped into invisible glass, which ends the magic world.

A witch came out of nowhere and said, 'Do you need help?'

Ellie said, 'Yes, I need to get home.'

The witch offered them her broom to fly away. Spencer and Ellie couldn't find their house but in the end they found it!

Zoë Balandis (7)

Archbishop Sumners Primary School, London

Scarlett's Magical Story

Spencer and Ellie went on a unicorn to Fairy Land! It was a beautiful place. They then went for a walk and were chatting merrily together. Soon there was a big shadow. What was it?

Suddenly, a huge dragon jumped out at them. Ellie was terrified. It roared, 'Come with me, you are going to be my dinner. I'm going to cook you and eat you all up!'

When the dragon said that Spencer shouted, 'Run!' They both ran for their lives. They both hated the dragon, especially Ellie. They ran and they ran until they saw an animal.

They found out that the animal was their unicorn. They jumped on and they went off to another place in Fairy Land. 'I didn't like that dragon,' said Ellie.

When they got there a witch came out. 'Come to my house little children.'

'No,' said Ellie, 'I know the story of Hansel and Gretel! You tried to eat them up so you can't force me.'

They took the broomstick and flew away with a screaming witch running after them. When they got home Ellie said, 'Thank you for taking me on a great adventure.'

Scarlett Matthews (7)

Archbishop Sumners Primary School, London

Chinayah's Magical Story

Ellie and Spencer went to a beautiful forest. Suddenly, a whisper came from the bushes. Nervously, a unicorn peered out of a prickly tree. Ellie realised that Isabelle the unicorn had hurt her leg.

Ellie placed a bandage as perfectly as a nurse on Isabelle. Bravely Spencer and Ellie rode determinedly on their magical adventure. From a far, dark distance appeared a ferocious dragon as long as the River Thames. Its teeth were as sharp as knives and its fire was as hot as the boiling sun. Spencer and Ellie dashed for shelter behind Isabelle. Isabelle's horns began to glow. Suddenly, a bright sparkly purple bubble appeared, so they jumped into the bubble where the fire could not reach the bubble.

They managed to get away but on their way they met a wicked, vicious witch called Victoria who yelled, 'Give me your magical, precious unicorn or else I will turn you both to gold dust!'

At that moment Isabelle turned into a flawless broom and galloped home like a graceful ballerina.

Finally, the magical adventure was over. Ellie and Spencer were back to the beautiful, peaceful forest.

Chinayah Martins-Manuel (6)

Archbishop Sumners Primary School, London

Nayher's Space Story

In space, Spencer took Ellie and her teddy to look around. After a long journey, they arrived on the moon.

They looked around and saw stars and decided to catch them while the stars were moving. Suddenly, an alien saw what Spencer and Ellie were doing with the stars.

The alien got on his spaceship and dragged Ellie and her teddy bear with him. She was worried about Spencer because he wasn't with her.

When Ellie was in the spaceship she was happy because she could see Spencer down on the moon. She waved at Spencer. The alien then waved to his friend.

Suddenly, they all looked down and saw a monster trying to eat them. The monster opened his mouth and his long tongue came out. Ellie was scared and she wanted to go home.

The alien had a brilliant idea, to take her home because she was scared the monster might eat her. She walked home safely and Spencer finished his adventure with the alien.

Nayher Gebrekidan (6)

Archbishop Sumners Primary School, London

Constance's Magical Story

Spencer and Ellie found themselves in a very hot, sunny place. Suddenly, they saw a golden horn peeking out from behind a tree and it was a... silky, soft unicorn!

A couple of minutes later they heard a loud roar. The unicorn was scared and ran away. They were terrified to see a fearsome dragon.

Burning hot flames were coming out of the dragon's mouth. Ellie's teddy bear was running away because he was frightened too.

They ran for their lives and they were so relieved to see the friendly unicorn. It carried them all to safety.

The unicorn led them to a witch. They weren't sure if she was kind or wicked. She gave Teddy a lolly and told Ellie and the elf, 'You can have one too.' The witch also gave them a broomstick so they could fly home at last. Ted had a very tiring journey and everyone was glad to be home.

Constance Lucia Palmer (6)
Archbishop Sumners Primary School, London

Ezekiel's Space Story

Spencer the elf held Ellie's wrist tightly as they flew into the night sky where the stars shone brightly. The Earth was a small dot in the distance of the dark beautiful sky.

After a long while they landed on Mars. It was a strange place. Whilst they were distracted by the amazing planet a green, funny-looking alien appeared.

All of a sudden the alien got into his spaceship and beamed Ellie and her teddy up into the green, shiny, transport pod.

Ellie and the alien took off in a flash into space to meet some other strange and unorthodox creatures.

Some had got crazy, slithery, long tongues, they looked different to anything or anyone you can meet on Earth!

At the end of a fascinating day they went home and Ellie said goodbye to her wonderful new friends until next time!

Ezekiel Gene Connolly (6)
Archbishop Sumners Primary School, London

Maya's Magical Story

Ellie and Spencer went on a unicorn ride.

A dragon came and it almost blew fire on them.

The dragon wanted to eat them but they ran away.

They wanted to go home.

A wicked witch came and tried to capture them.

They then stole the broom and flew back to Ellie's house. What an adventure!

Maya Brookes

Archbishop Sumners Primary School, London

I'sha's Magical Story

Ellie and Spencer flew off to a faraway land where no one would find them, except... a dragon who was starving and wanted to eat some children! They ran away as fast as they could and they made it.

They promised they would never go there again and so they never did.

Then they saw an ugly old lady who wanted their unicorn, they traded it for her fast flying broomstick and they took off.

They flew all the way home so Ellie could go to bed. She fell into bed and went right back to sleep.

I'sha Amara Elaine Barletey (7)

Archbishop Sumners Primary School, London

Efe's Jungle Story

Two children and one bear were swinging in a forest and they were having a great time.
After a while the children saw a snake and the little girl was very afraid.
The two children and the bear ran.
After that the two children and the bear saw a lion and they were scared.
Suddenly the lion gave a ride to the boy and the girl, also the bear home. It was a friendly lion.
Finally, the boy and girl, also the bear, swung home. When the children got home they were really excited to tell their lovely adventure to their parents and their friends. After a while when they started telling their exciting adventure, everyone was listening to them in absolute silence.
When their parents heard about the lion and the snake they worried if something had happened to the children, also they were surprised. The parents were patiently waiting for children to stop talking. Finally the children stopped talking, so straight away mum asked if they were alright. When she got the answer of, 'Yes Mum we are okay,' Mum and Dad were very happy and they lived happily forever.

Efe Atanasov (6)
Chesterton Primary School, London

Max's Jungle Story

Ellie and Spencer were at the most famous jungle in the world. It was the most unusual jungle because when it was morning the stars were out but when it was evening the sun was shining.
Ellie was puzzled because day was night and night was day. 'Can we see all the wonderful animals?' said Ellie.
'Yes we can,' replied Spencer.
The first animal they met was a fierce snake, he said, 'Tu-whit tu-whoo!'
'What a weird snake,' said Ellie.
'Everything is backwards!' said Spencer.
Suddenly, a friendly lion popped out. He said, 'Pretty Polly.' Ellie and Spencer were surprised. 'My name is Pretty Polly. I will Pretty Polly you home.'
Finally they swung on banana-flavoured vines to get themselves home.

Max Stephens (6)
Chesterton Primary School, London

Hiba's Jungle Story

First Ellie and Spencer the elf went to have an adventure around the dark jungle.

Next they saw a slippery, skinny snake. 'Can I go with you for an adventure?' he asked.

'Nooo!' they both said.

Then they felt scared and they ran away.

After that they met a huge lion. 'Can I go with you to have a wild adventure?' he asked.

'Yes you can,' they both said.

Later on they climbed on the lion's back and they had fun travelling around the wild jungle.

Finally they went back home and had a rest.

Hiba Boukhari (6)
Chesterton Primary School, London

Adam's Jungle Story

Soon Ellie and Spencer arrived at the big and dark jungle. As they were swinging on the long green vines they noticed that there was another living thing in the jungle, it was a cute bear.

After that they found a very naughty snake. They wanted to ask him to help with finding the King of the Jungle.

Sadly the angry snake refused to answer the question and said, 'I'm never going to tell you and I'm very hungry now!'

While they were running away from the snake, Ellie spotted a lion. They asked him, 'Where is the King of the Jungle?'

He said, 'I'm the King of the Jungle! Would you like me to show you around?'

'Yes please,' they said so off they went.

Soon it became dark and Ellie had to go home.

Adam Guermane (5)

Chesterton Primary School, London

Dionne's Jungle Story

Soon Ellie and Spencer arrived at a tropical island swinging on green vines with Ellie's teddy called Shimmer.

When they were on a strong branch they met a talking snake called Evil Nasty. He was the size of five wardrobes!

They then found out that it was an evil snake because of his evil grin and his red fiery eyes so they all ran away quickly.

After escaping the evil snake they met a friendly lion called Leo, but at first they were worried because they thought the lion was going to eat them.

Leo gave them a friendly smile and they knew they could trust him to help them home safely because he was the king of the whole jungle.

They rode on Leo's back to the green vines and swung all the way back home and fell fast asleep in bed.

Dionne Malachi Fraser (6)

Chesterton Primary School, London

Aiman's Jungle Story

First Jack and Jill, also Teddy, went on an adventure in the jungle and swung on the vines high in the trees, getting higher and higher.

Next they saw a big, big, big and long, long, long snake and they were scared. They stood still like a statue.

Suddenly, the snake scared them and they ran as fast as they could and were safe.

They met a lion and Teddy was a bit scared. The lion was not rude at all, also the lion said hello and they were all surprised.

After that the lion took them out of the dark scary jungle fast, they were happy and they were safe and went out safely.

At last they reached home and they were happy about their adventure. They went home safely and nicely, also it was night-time.

Aiman Abdu Ahmed (6)

Chesterton Primary School, London

Murad's Jungle Story

... at the rainforest in Madagascar. Ellie and Spencer met lots of charming koala bears. They had lots of fun.

From there they flew to the jungles of India. Once the friends were nearly eaten by a giant boa, but luckily they got away.

The giant snake chased them for a mile. However, our friends escaped from the boa who was distracted by cheeky monkeys.

Spencer and Ellie found themselves in the bushes facing an enormous lion called Saheeb. He was really friendly.

Saheeb gave Spencer and Ellie a ride all the way to the Taj Mahal. The children were impressed with its beauty.

As the day came to an end, the children flew back home to finish their homework and prepare for bed.

Murad Agazade (6)
Chesterton Primary School, London

Antonio's Jungle Story

The fairy went to Ellie's house then they went to the jungle and they got to swing on vines. Then they jumped off and started to walk.

They stopped walking and they saw a snake. Ellie was scared, they went backwards.

They ran and ran so fast. They got tired and they couldn't run anymore.

They walked then they stopped and saw a lion, it was looking at them. They thought that the lion was going to eat them but it didn't.

They got a happy ride, it was so happy they became friends with the lion. They then jumped off. They swung on the vines and they went to Ellie's house. Ellie then went to bed.

Antonio Ross-Hamilton (6)

Chesterton Primary School, London

Safwan's Jungle Story

Ellie and Spencer went to the jungle, they were swinging, then they met Teddy, a nice little bear.
A snake came along, a venomous snake! It started to get close to Ellie but in the nick of time Spencer the elf pushed Ellie.
They ran as fast as they could but Ellie tripped. Although Spencer was tired he got Ellie to safety.
They saw a big, hairy, scary lion with big eyes and it said, 'Come on my back.'
They were riding on the lion's back. They were riding all day. When it got to Ellie's bedtime they went to Ellie's house.
Ellie then swung home to bed.

Safwan Elmi (6)
Chesterton Primary School, London

Tiana's Jungle Story

Ellie and Spencer flew to Battersea Park at night to have some fun because the park was quiet at night.

As they started playing they saw a big glowing snake in the middle of the green grass in the park. They started to run away from the big glowing snake.

As they were running away from the snake they saw a big tiger hiding in the bushes.

The tiger told them to hop on his back and he would take them to safety.

As they reached a safe place, Ellie and Spencer got back on their flying stick and flew back home.

Tiana Oleyede (6)
Chesterton Primary School, London

Zakiyah's Jungle Story

Ellie and Spencer were swinging on vines. Spencer and Ellie were having an adventure.

Ellie and Spencer got shocked because there was a snake, it was an anaconda and it was in their way!

Ellie and Spencer were running out of the jungle home.

Up came a lion to take Ellie and Spencer home.

Ellie and Spencer were happy to go home and Ellie could go back in her nice warm bed.

Ellie said goodbye then Ellie asked if they could go on another adventure again.

Zakiyah Hamir Mohamed (6)
Chesterton Primary School, London

Samuel's Jungle Story

Ellie, Spencer and the teddy were swinging on vines in the jungle and having fun.
When they stopped they met a snake and the snake was not friendly.
Ellie, Spencer and the teddy started to run away from the snake. The snake was staring at them.
They kept running, then they met a lion, it was a bit scary. It looked at them in a scary way.
They then became friends and he helped them by carrying them on his back.
They went back home on the ropes.

Samuel Mireku (6)

Chesterton Primary School, London

Isabella's Jungle Story

Ellie and Spencer went to South America and they were swinging on the vines like very cheeky monkeys that liked bananas.

Suddenly, there was a bad snake, he was very hungry and he was about to eat the kids.

They got scared but then the snake was almost about to eat the kids.

A lion jumped out of the bushes and saved them.

The lion made friends with them.

They then glided home and the kids never forgot the lion.

Isabella Ashpitel (6)

Chesterton Primary School, London

Amelia's Jungle Story

Once there was a jungle and dangerous animals lived there. One of the dangerous animals was hungry and it ate a monkey.

Next there was a terrifying snake and he suddenly tangled himself up.

Next the snake untangled itself and went up a tree, it was his home.

The snake met a lion and the lion wanted to eat the snake.

After that the snake scared the lion away.

Finally it was time for the animals to go to bed.

Amelia Ashpitel (6)
Chesterton Primary School, London

Elijah's Jungle Story

In the jungle Ellie and Spencer saw a little bear. They were swinging on tree vines. They had so much fun.

Ellie and Spencer were walking through the jungle when they saw a slithery snake with his tongue sticking out.

The snake tried to grab Ellie and they ran away.

Next they bumped into a friendly lion.

Afterwards, the lion gave them a ride.

Finally, Ellie and Spencer swung their way back home.

Elijah Quartey (6)
Chesterton Primary School, London

Callum's Jungle Story

Ellie and Spencer were swinging through the magical forest feeling excited.

Soon they found a king snake who told them to be careful.

Then the snake tried to eat them so they ran as fast as a scared cheetah.

They found a lion who said, 'Do you want to come with me?'

The lion showed them the magical jungle.

They finally swung through the jungle and jumped into bed before anyone noticed.

Callum Campbell-Mackay (6)
Chesterton Primary School, London

Sofia's Jungle Story

First Ellie and Spencer went to swing on vines and it was fun to do.

Next they met an evil snake that was coiled all around his branches. The snake was so smooth. Then the snake scared the children away.

After that they met a happy lion.

On the next day the happy lion gave the children a ride.

Finally they swung back home to have dinner, breakfast and lunch.

Sofia Rosa Robinson (6)

Chesterton Primary School, London

Elisabeth's Jungle Story

Ellie and Spencer were flying through the jungle in the trees on vines.

They saw a big boa snake that was about to eat them...

They ran away as fast as they could.

Then, out of nowhere popped out a lion. He wasn't bad, he was friendly and big.

He let them have a piggyback ride all the way through the jungle.

They then flew on the vines back home.

Elisabeth Zemskov (6)
Chesterton Primary School, London

Ashton's Jungle Story

Ellie and Spencer were in a jungle.

They saw a snake.

They ran away.

Next they saw a lion.

They rode on the lion.

They went back home.

Ashton Savva Burrowes (5)

Chesterton Primary School, London

Abdullah's Jungle Story

First they went to the jungle to explore and the girl brought her teddy bear with her.

Next they saw a big snake. The kids were scared and ran away from the snake.

They saw a big lion. The lion told them that he was King of the Jungle. The lion said, 'You can stay with me and we can have lunch together.'

In the evening, the kids said, 'We want to go home.' The lion took the kids to their house.

Finally the kids swung on the branches and they jumped through the window quietly and went to sleep and they lived happily ever after.

Abdullah Rayyan (6)
Chesterton Primary School, London

Jack's Jungle Story

Lilly, Max (the teddy bear) and Lucky swung on the vines and saw birds in the sky flying quickly.

They landed on a huge and thick branch. They explored the branch and bumped into a very scary snake. 'That is a very scary snake!' said Max.

'Look!' said Lilly. 'The s-s-snake is t-t-trying to e-e-eat us!'

'U-u-u-us!' said Lucky.

'Yes, us!' replied Lilly.

'We must run!' explained Max in a squeaky voice.

They met a lion which turned out to be good. They hid from the snake with the lion. They hid behind some thorny leaves.

'We need a plan before the snake comes back,' said the lion in a deep voice.

'I know, if you don't mind Lion,' said Lucky, 'we need to ride on your back.'

'Of course,' said the lion, so off they went.

They swung on the same vines to go back home.

'Bye-bye,' called the elf and Max turned back into a soft toy again.

Jack Hugo de Piro O'Connell (7)

Thomas's Academy, London

Ghaliyah's Magical Story

Soon Ellie and Spencer had arrived at a magical land full of unicorns and then they had found a unicorn! The unicorn was trying to talk to them but just then Spencer remembered that he could speak to the unicorn! The unicorn said, 'Hello my name is Uina. I need help battling a dragon!'

'Let's go then!' said Ellie and Spencer, so off they went. They got there and Uina left them.

Then, all of a sudden, Ellie started to feel frightened, but Spencer just magicked up some weapons and had a battle and they had won!

The dragon wasn't defeated yet! They ran as fast as they could to save themselves and their lives from being burnt and crumbled into thousands of bits!

Just then Uina came back and said, 'Ha. Well you might succeed next time.'

'Sorry,' said everyone.

'Now I'm going to take you somewhere!'

'Argh!' screamed Ellie so loudly that the witch came out of her candy-made house with her broomstick.

Ellie was so, so, so scared that she snatched her broomstick off her.
Everyone then hopped on the broomstick and flew off home peacefully.

Ghaliyah Esmail (7)

Thomas's Academy, London

Oscyra's Magical Story

Ellie and Spencer went on a pony so that they could go to the castle quickly.

On the way a dragon was breathing fire, it was scary.

The dragon started to chase Ellie and Spencer. Ellie was frightened. Spencer said, 'Don't worry.'

The pony saved them and the pony took them to a candy house.

A witch was there, she said, 'What do you want?'

'Nothing,' Spencer said.

'Then why are you here?'

'Because a pony brought us here. Can you take us home?'

'Sure,' said the witch.

They were taken home by her broom. 'It was a magical time!' said Ellie.

Oscyra Moses (7)

Thomas's Academy, London

Channai's Magical Story

Ellie and Spencer went to a magical castle, they flew there. Outside the castle there was a beautiful unicorn.

A fearsome dragon came and it was breathing fire at the children, they were very scared, even Spencer, he was supposed to be brave not scared. The dragon was breathing too much fire so the children ran. They worried so much and Ellie was screaming so much.

When they got rid of the dragon they went to the castle and on the way they saw a unicorn so they went on it, it was scary at first but in the end it was fine.

Afterwards, they saw the unicorn. They kept on walking and they saw a wicked witch, she gave the children one wish.

The wish was to use her broom to get home. They were not afraid anymore. 'Yes,' Ellie said.

'We are home!' said Spencer.

Channai Chambers (7)

Thomas's Academy, London

Malakai's Jungle Story

When Spencer and Ellie got there they played on the trees for one minute to start the fun in the jungle.

They saw Skinny the snake and Spencer said, 'It's okay, he's a hissy snake.'

He said, 'I'm called Skinny.'

They nearly got eaten up by the snake so they ran away from them.

Ellie said, 'Who's that Mr Lion? He's definitely kind.'

He took them round the jungle.

They went swinging then they went back home.

Malakai Maxwell-Roberts (7)

Thomas's Academy, London

Natalja's Magical Story

Ellie and Spencer rode on a beautiful, pink, purple and white unicorn because Ellie had never been on a real amazing unicorn and Spencer wanted a ride. They both saw a very fierce dragon. It nearly burnt Ellie but Spencer quickly moved Ellie back without hurting the adorable teddy bear.

Next they had to run away from the frightening dragon because he was about to eat Ellie, Spencer and Teddy Bear. 'Oh no!' said Ellie and Spencer. After, they rode on the very pretty unicorn again. It felt like a long time but it was only half an hour. Then Ellie said, 'I like the unicorn,' and Spencer laughed.

After that they came to a witch's home, she nearly put a spell on Ellie but Spencer used his powers to stop the evil wicked witch!

Finally they set off for Ellie's beautiful and lovely house and Ellie went fast asleep dreaming about where they were going tomorrow.

Natalja Gilles (7)
Thomas's Academy, London

Zaynab's Magical Story

When Spencer and Ellie landed they ended up in a magical forest. They walked through the beautiful forest and saw a unicorn so they both rode on the unicorn.

As soon as they got off the unicorn it turned into a fierce dragon! They were so scared that they ran away so quickly.

As soon as they ran they nearly fell down and they soon couldn't see the dragon. Ellie was frightened that the dragon would eat her teddy.

When they got over a really huge mountain the dragon turned back to a unicorn. Ellie thought the unicorn was so cute.

When the unicorn was tired Spencer and Ellie jumped off and they went to Candy Land. They saw a witch and made friends with them.

She let Spencer and Ellie go on her broom and Spencer took Ellie home on the broomstick.

Zaynab Abouchouche (7)

Thomas's Academy, London

Elias' Jungle Story

Ellie and Spencer flew quickly and safely to the refreshing jungle. Ellie was, of course, frightened 100% so Spencer held on to her tightly so she wouldn't panic.

Suddenly, when they got to the lovely jungle, they stopped. There was a snake! They were both scared. Spencer said, 'Don't touch.'

Ellie said, 'Run,' so Ellie and Spencer ran and, phew, they got away and it was very serious.

After that they went to another place in the jungle. They saw a lion looking at them.

They never knew but the tiger was actually friendly and soon they were playing all around the beautiful jungle.

Finally the lion took them to the end of the jungle. Spencer and Ellie were then swinging on trees and when they got home they slept.

Elias Oualah (7)
Thomas's Academy, London

Alex's Jungle Story

Ellie and Spencer went to the jungle and saw lots of animals like lions, tigers and penguins. They swung off the branch and had so much fun.

They saw a snake, they couldn't get past the snake so they went back to go and see the elf and ran past the snake.

They kept on walking to find a different animal like a lion.

They found a lion that was scary and ran as far as they could. They then found a monkey that was crying and they helped.

The lion ran as fast as he could to greet them so they played and had a great time.

They swung back home to get back to sleep with their mother and father. They had a great breakfast.

Alex Edward Thorne (7)
Thomas's Academy, London

Inas' Magical Story

At Kind Land there was a beautiful unicorn. She was lonely so Ellie and Spencer got on her back and it was so fun!

The unicorn took them to a dragon and they were so scared.

They ran as fast as they could because he was breathing fire.

Then the unicorn saved them. She took them to another place.

It was a witch's house. They were even more scared than before. 'Oh no!' They thought she was a bad witch.

She was a kind witch and she let Ellie and Spencer use her magic broom that could make them fly so they both went back home.

Inas Khelfaoui (7)

Thomas's Academy, London

Amir's Jungle Story

Spencer and Ellie had gone to the jungle and they had a swing entrance. They found a baby bear and they played with the bear.

Next they landed on a branch and met a snake called Guled.

They found out that the snake was bold so they ran away as fast as they could and escaped in time.

They then met a lion called Max, it was nice and took them around the whole jungle.

They headed to the house before Ellie's parents got back.

They got home and she went to sleep.

Amir Mohamoud (7)
Thomas's Academy, London

Adomas' Space Story

'We are in outer space!' cried Ellie. They were in the air and it was freezing. 'Brrr,' said Ellie, 'it's cold here.'

'I see a planet called Pluto,' said Spencer.

When they were collecting stars an alien was at the back of them but they were too busy collecting stars to notice.

Suddenly, her teddy was floating. 'Teddy!' cried Ellie, she was floating too. 'Oh no,' she got sucked into a UFO. 'Hello,' said Ellie to the alien.

'Hello,' said the alien back.

Suddenly she was zooming past the stars. 'Can I have a turn please?' said Ellie.

'OK,' said the alien.

When they were out of petrol a slimy eight-legged, three-eyed and 10 metre tongued alien appeared. 'Argh!' cried Ellie. 'It's a scary monster!'

They got away. Ellie was sleepy so Spencer and the alien took her home. On the way they crashed into Mars and then they crashed in Ellie's garden. They both said bye to Ellie and they lived happily ever after.

Adomas Mucinskas (7)
Trinity St Mary's CE Primary School, London

Renan's Jungle Story

Ellie and Spencer were in space. Ellie said to Spencer, 'Can we play there?'
'Yes,' said Spencer.
Ellie saw a snake and the snake said, 'Do you want to play?'
Ellie said, 'No!' and the snake squeezed Ellie.
They ran away from the scary snake.
They found a lion and the lion asked, 'Do you want to ride on my back? Where would you like to go?'
'Please can we go home?'
They soon arrived home.

Renan Carias (7)
Trinity St Mary's CE Primary School, London

Zahra's Magical Story

Ellie couldn't believe her eyes! They were in Magic Land. There were magic gloves and talking trees, it was amazing! They found a talking unicorn and she asked, 'Do you want a ride?' They took the ride and appeared in another part of the land.

It was Dragon Land! A dragon tried to burn them and the unicorn was gone.

They ran as fast as they could and they finally lost the dragon. It was really scary because the dragon had sharp teeth, a red body and green hair.

They found the unicorn again. The unicorn flew to another place where there was lots of candy.

They stopped there and the very nice witch gave them sweets. The witch said, 'Do you want a ride?' 'Yes,' they said.

They got a brown magical broomstick and they went home.

Zahra Fatema Khimani (7)
Trinity St Mary's CE Primary School, London

Elijah's Space Story

Seven months later when Ellie opened her eyes she was in space and she saw lots of stars. Ellie could not believe her eyes, Ellie was happy.

Spencer asked Ellie, 'Do you want to go on an exciting adventure?'

Ellie said, 'Of course.' Spencer and Ellie started to count all the stars they could see and they counted 27 stars.

Then Ellie noticed a cheeky alien, the alien put Ellie and Teddy into the alien's ship. Spencer was already in the ship making a cup of tea.

Then Ellie noticed that the alien wasn't that cheeky and the aliens were just giving a tour of space.

After that, a monster appeared with eight tentacles and everyone was shocked the monster had a long tongue.

The alien dropped Ellie home.

Elijah Marley Walker (7)
Trinity St Mary's CE Primary School, London

Dougal's Space Story

Finally, Ellie and Spencer got to space, it was amazing, there were so many stars and Earth looked so far away! They could see so many planets and they were flying.

They started looking at the stars, they were counting them. Suddenly, Spencer started picking them. 'Why are you picking the stars?' Ellie said. Before Spencer could answer he spotted an alien. Suddenly Ellie and Spencer started floating up. They looked up and realised they were being sucked up by a UFO. Ellie felt very scared.

It turned out that the alien was Spencer's best friend who wanted to help get Ellie home. He also let Ellie steer. Ellie thought it was an amazing view from in the UFO!

Unexpectedly a monster appeared with 12 legs, it was green and it had three eyes. Luckily, Spencer threw a star at it and it ran away.

In the end Ellie had to go home. She said, 'Goodbye Spencer, goodbye alien!' Then she went home thinking what an amazing adventure she had.

Dougal Hamilton (7)

Trinity St Mary's CE Primary School, London

David's Space Story

One day Ellie opened her eyes and she couldn't believe it, she was in space! She saw tons of dazzling, bright golden stars.

'Do you want to collect some stars and take one home?' asked Spencer.

'OK,' answered Ellie as they collected some stars. While they collected some stars Ellie saw Teddy floating in the air. They went to get Teddy back but suddenly they were both floating and found a strange-looking green alien with two antennae on its head.

They flew everywhere in space and explored the planets and collected lots of awesome items.

All of a sudden, a yellow three-eyed alien with twelve green, slimy tentacles and an orange head with more than one thousand teeth and a frog's tongue tried to attack them. The green alien then activated the laser guns and killed the bad alien.

David Oyat Loum (7)
Trinity St Mary's CE Primary School, London

Hirad's Pirate Story

Ellie and Spencer were sailing on a boat in a vast ocean only with a tiny island in sight. 'When will we get there?' asked Ellie.

Ellie couldn't believe her eyes as in front of her was a treasure chest. *This might be full of gold*, thought Ellie.

Suddenly, a pirate appeared out of nowhere! 'This treasure is mine!' said the captain. Ellie and Spencer were frightened.

'Walk the plank, you scurvy rat!' said the captain. Ellie and Spencer had to accept the risk and without caution, Spencer walked the plank.

Eventually, the time each of them walked the plank, they were already on a dolphin and zooming through the waves of the sea.

In the end, Ellie and Spencer were walking home. 'We escaped!' said Ellie, realising her and Spencer had pirate hats.

Hirad Baghi (7)

Trinity St Mary's CE Primary School, London

Natalia's Magical Story

Ellie suddenly opened her eyes and she saw a unicorn with a rainbow horn, pink body and a long tail. The unicorn let them have a ride.

Suddenly, there was a scaly dragon and the unicorn ran away. The dragon burnt the grass behind them, he wanted to eat them.

They ran for their lives and they nearly got burnt but they dived in a bush. The dragon went home because he didn't see them in the bush.

They came out of the fat bush and the unicorn came and they had more fun.

Suddenly, a beautiful witch appeared, she seemed to be a nice witch. She gave them her broomstick and said, 'You can use my broomstick to go home.' They went home on the yellow broomstick. They loved their adventure but they had to go to sleep.

Natalia Paluch (7)

Trinity St Mary's CE Primary School, London

Christian's Space Story

Ellie and Spencer explored around the extraordinary universe. There were thousands and millions of stars around them! They were amazed. They both started collecting stars for science back on Earth. 'This is awesome!' Spencer said, but what they didn't know was that there might be an alien plotting evil plans!
Suddenly an alien collected them in his ship.
Ellie was scared.
They soon found out the alien was friendly.
Spencer was horrified upon seeing the monster.
Suddenly, an alien frog monster appeared. The alien communicated with the crazy alien and told him that they were going to Earth.
The alien took Ellie home. She said, 'Thank you.'
Then she said, 'Goodnight.'

Christian Jermaine Pottinger (7)
Trinity St Mary's CE Primary School, London

Brooke's Magical Story

They appeared on a magical island and they saw singing flowers, lollipop trees and a unicorn. The unicorn said, 'Do you want a ride?' and the unicorn galloped off with them.

Suddenly, the unicorn threw them off and ran away. Just at that moment they saw a giant dragon.

They ran as fast as they could. They felt the burning on their legs.

Then, they saw a unicorn. They got on her back but the unicorn got lost and ran away.

Afterwards they saw a witch. At first they were a bit unsure whether she was good or bad.

Finally the witch gave them her broomstick and they flew home.

Brooke Humphreys (7)
Trinity St Mary's CE Primary School, London

Elioenai's Magical Story

Ellie could not believe her eyes, Ellie and Spencer travelled to a magical land. Ellie was surprised! She saw a unicorn!
Ellie was so scared because a big, fiery dragon came hovering around Ellie and Spencer the elf. Ellie and Spencer the elf ran as fast as their legs could carry them in a huge amount of fright. Luckily, the unicorn came to help Spencer the elf and Ellie.
Suddenly, a kind witch came and said, 'Do you need some help?' in a screeching voice. She let them use her broom.
Ellie and Spencer were safe and sound because the witch let them use her broom.

Elioenai Gordon (6)
Trinity St Mary's CE Primary School, London

Ratib's Pirate Story

One sunny day Ellie and Spencer the elf decided to go on an adventure on an oak boat.
In the corner of Ellie's eye she saw a shiny gold chest with gold coins splattering out. It was a chest!
Suddenly, a mean, grumpy pirate appeared. 'That's my treasure,' he yelled. He wrapped them up and pushed them somewhere.
'It's the plank!' Ellie yelled but the pirate forced them so Spencer went first.
In a splash the dolphins caught them and they rode on them home. What fun they had.
Finally, they reached home. 'What an adventure!'

Ratib Mulindwa Kalikka (6)
Trinity St Mary's CE Primary School, London

Eden's Magical Story

Ellie couldn't believe her eyes, they landed on a magical land. There were singing trees. Out of nowhere a unicorn appeared and it said, 'Come and have a ride on me!'

Suddenly, a humongous dragon appeared and the unicorn put them down but the dragon wanted them for dinner.

They ran as fast as their legs could carry them. The dragon was gaining on them. Ellie was so scared. The unicorn came and rescued them.

Suddenly, a great old witch appeared in the shadows.

She leant them her broom to go home.

Eden Shalom (7)

Trinity St Mary's CE Primary School, London

Noah's Space Story

Ellie and the elf travelled to space. Ellie was so excited until they were on the moon and she thought she was going to explode!
Ellie and Spencer were collecting the stars.
Suddenly, someone or should I say an alien was invading and Ellie was picked up by a UFO!
They were floating and driving somewhere on a planet.
They found a monster, they used a laser to make it go away.
Soon Ellie was home and she was very happy.

Noah Destalem (7)
Trinity St Mary's CE Primary School, London

Alexander's Pirate Story

Ellie was going on a boat and then Ellie and Spencer were on the island.

They found treasure, then they saw a pirate ship and there was a pirate.

They saw a pirate and the pirate said, 'This is my treasure!' The pirate sang a song.

They walked on a plank, they fell into the sea. They were scared. The dolphins came.

The dolphins took them to their home.

They were walking to their home. They were on the beach.

Alexander Kolbuc (7)

Trinity St Mary's CE Primary School, London

Mikayla's Pirate Story

Ellie went with Spencer to go to an island and were rowing a boat to get there.

They arrived at the island and found a piece of shiny treasure.

They met a pirate with a sword trying to get the treasure so he could have it.

They had to walk the plank because the pirate wanted the treasure.

They rode on whales to get home, they were diving through the river.

They got home, held hands and walked home together.

Mikayla Hornsby-Odoi

Trinity St Mary's CE Primary School, London

Franek's Jungle Story

In the forgotten jungle a new adventure was just about to begin. Ellie and Spencer leapt from vine to vine, looking at the damp jungle beneath them. Suddenly, they saw a humongous, ferocious and dangerous snake. Although they were a bit scared they wanted to befriend this massive creature. Soon they realised he was a poisonous reptile who wanted to harm them so they ran away!

The children and their magical talking teddy thought they were really, really, really lucky to be alive, that's for sure!

They then met a very kind and generous lion and asked him if he could give them a quick ride so they could escape from the snake. The lion said, 'Yes I can little children, hop on!' The lion ran as fast as lightning. They knew they could trust the lion from the moment they met him by his kind smile.

The lion took them to the edge of the jungle where there was a lake with piranhas in. It was almost night-time. They swung on some more vines to get over the lake that was 2.8 metres deep. Finally after their long and eventful day, they saw their house. It was good to be back home. They had had enough adventures for one day!

Franek Wielogorski (7)

Westminster Cathedral RC Primary School, London

Mateusz's Jungle Story

One night Ellie was woken by a tapping on her window. It was Spencer the elf. He said, 'Do you want to go on an adventure?' Where did they go? They went to a scary, beautiful jungle.

The jungle was all covered in huge, big wet leaves. They walked a little bit and a snake appeared. The huge snake said, 'What are you doing here? Would you like to play with me?'

They said, 'No thank you.'

'I think he wants to eat us,' Spencer said. They walked away from him.

Suddenly they saw a sad-looking tiger. They said, 'What's the matter?' to the tiger.

'I do not have any friends.'

'We could be your friends.'

'Oh yes please,' said the joyful tiger.

'But you have to give us a ride,' Ellie said.

'Okay,' said the tiger.

They saw all the animals but it was time to go home. They swung on branches to Ellie's comfy home.

Mateusz Krol (6)
Westminster Cathedral RC Primary School, London

Ruby-Belle's Jungle Story

Ellie and Spencer swung quickly across the green vines, they had arrived at the damp, huge jungle. It looked calm like a calm snail but loads of animals filled the zoo.

All of a sudden a dotted red snake stared at Spencer, Ellie and the teddy! They didn't know what to do so they stood still and watched the snake stare at them.

'Argh!' shouted Ellie. Spencer ran as fast as he could. Ellie followed then Teddy followed. The snake went after them but they hid in a bush.

'Hello, my name is Oscar the kind lion.'

'My name is Ellie, this is Spencer and this is Teddy.'

'Nice to meet you, do you want a ride home?'

'Yes.'

'Come on then.' So Ellie, Spencer and Teddy hopped on the lion and in a flash, Oscar said, 'Bye,' and put them on the green vines.

'Bye Oscar,' they said as they raced away.

They swung on the green vines and carefully they got off and jogged home. Ellie invited Spencer in to have a roast dinner!

Ruby-Belle Sweeney (7)

Westminster Cathedral RC Primary School, London

Alexandra's Jungle Story

Once upon a time there was an elf called Spencer and there was a girl called Ellie. They were very best friends so they went on an adventure together in the jungle.

When they got there they saw a brown and green snake which had a long, red, slimy tongue. When they said hello the snake hissed very, very loud. After that Ellie and Spencer ran away because both of them were terribly frightened and very scared.

Afterwards they met a lion and luckily when they said hello the lion was so nice and said, 'Would you like to have a ride?'

They said, 'Yes.'

When they rode on the friendly lion the lion said very nicely, 'Where would you like to go?'

Spencer and Ellie said, 'We would like to go to Cornwall.' So the lion took them there.

After that the kids swung back home on the long green and fun vines and they lived happily ever after.

Alexandra Maria Taylor (6)
Westminster Cathedral RC Primary School, London

Lisa's Jungle Story

Ellie and Spencer went to a colourful strange jungle. When Ellie the bright, kind, lovely girl was in the jungle she lost Spencer the elf! Luckily, Ellie met a bear and they both worked together to find Spencer. When they found Spencer they were playing happily.

When they were climbing trees they met a strange snake who was very angry so he chased Ellie and Spencer to the snake's terrifying home.

When they were in the snake's home it tried to eat them but Ellie, Spencer and the little bear smacked it on the cheek. They then ran away with all their might.

Ellie and Spencer weren't looking and they fell onto the floppy lion and it quickly stood up. The lion asked them, 'Why on earth are you far away in the jungle?' The children whispered why.

Ellie asked, 'Please can you take us home?'

The lion thought for a minute and said, 'Well yes I can,' and he leapt them across like a buzz of electricity zooming.

When they got home they went into their little tree house and decided to sleep there. They had a lovely dinner with lovely dessert that was strawberry pie.

Lisa Leese (7)
Westminster Cathedral RC Primary School, London

Daniella's Jungle Story

One stormy night there was a worried girl called Ellie. She was woken up by a tapping noise at her window: *tap, tap, tap*. It was Spencer the elf! Spencer said to Ellie, 'Would you like to go on an exciting adventure?'

They flew high above the high rooftops, it was so, so scary. Soon they had arrived at the wonderful rainforest! Ellie and Spencer were swinging everywhere. They thought they were monkeys. Ellie was definitely enjoying herself because she had never done it before. In the first place she was worried but now she was swinging like mad.

When they landed and started to walk, they saw something that was gigantic... Spencer was shocked! He said to himself, 'Why is the massive snake so big?' Spencer said to Ellie, 'I think it's better if we carry on or better to run.'

Ellie agreed. Ellie said, 'Run!' The girl said, 'I think this is a hungry anaconda and I think she wants to eat us!'

They started to speed up and were running like a cheetah. They ran so fast! The tiny little bear was really stretching his short legs, he nearly did the splits! Ellie couldn't believe it because she had never done the splits before.

They stopped for a little second and they saw a very kind lion. The lion even let the kids ride on its back and the lion took the kids to the treetops. Ellie loved the treetops, she thought it was her favourite thing but she did like riding on a lion. What she loved was being with Spencer, she had never seen an elf before. Ellie said to Spencer, 'It's like a dream come true!' Ellie loved meeting new people. Then she remembered to give Spencer a hug and say thank you.

She remembered all the trees around the bear, Ellie and Spencer. 'It's like we are living in the jungle and there are monkeys everywhere!' she said. Ellie saw the little trees near her house. Ellie shouted to the bear and Spencer, 'There's our house!' Then it was the end of the day.

Daniella Ortiz Posso (7)
Westminster Cathedral RC Primary School, London

Bobby's Jungle Story

Ellie and Spencer swung wildly on the spiky vines, they saw lots of different animals.

They came across a mischievous snake and he said he wanted some company so they stayed.

They didn't trust the snake when he said, 'I'm going to have raw humans for dinner!'

They then met a smiley lion called Harry. He said, 'Ride on my back.'

They said, 'Alright.'

Harry was really happy when he had company. He said, 'This is the best day of my life.'

Finally, they swung back home really happily, they were just in time for tea.

Bobby Barnes (6)
Westminster Cathedral RC Primary School, London

Marvel's Jungle Story

Once upon a time Ellie and Spencer were swinging through the bright spooky woods.

Ellie and Spencer saw a giant snake. Ellie and Spencer said, 'What should we do?'

'Let's run away quickly.'

'OK, what should we do?'

'Run away until we get down off the tree.'

They saw a lion, he was really kind. The children were really happy.

Spencer then said, 'Bye Ellie, go back to bed!'

Marvel Yao Ashvin Sebastien N'zi (7)
Westminster Cathedral RC Primary School, London

Julia Maire's Jungle Story

Ellie the adventurous girl found a wild jungle as big as the Amazon. They swung on the long dusty dead vines and crashed on the decaying leaves. Some animals were a little bit frightening but they ignored them.

They landed on the damp and hard ground. When they were walking it was a deadly place. Once they felt tired they stopped and in front of them was a snake! The snake had a long colourful body.

All of a sudden, the snake that had a family which was evil, looked at them and Ellie didn't like it. The look on its devious face looked like it wanted to eat them alive! The friendly bear, silly elf and Ellie the sports girl ran but the snake slithered after them.

Next they heard a bush rattle like a baby's toy and they were scared what would come out. Ellie the playful girl went further out from the rattly, noisy bush.

They saw a lion, he was friendly and the lion smiled. The lion did not look like other lions. The friendly lion said, 'Would it be nice to take you home?'

When the lion took them off of his back they swung on another vine. Then Ellie said goodbye! Silly Spencer would really miss kind Ellie.

Julia Maire Dela Cuesta (7)

Westminster Cathedral RC Primary School, London

Jessica's Jungle Story

Ellie and the funny elf called Spencer went in the fun and humongous jungle! They swung quickly and excitedly on the vines because they loved swinging on the vines.

When they finished swinging on the vines, all of a sudden they saw a creepy, wide and rude snake trying to get them and devour them slowly because this poisonous snake liked children.

Ellie quickly grabbed onto the cute teddy and they ran scaredly. Ellie was trembling with fear. Spencer was worried because the snake might eat them.

They were running quickly, then they stopped because they saw a lion that said, 'Do you want to have a ride?' Ellie, Spencer and Teddy went on the beautiful and fantastic lion.

They stopped at the vines because it was the first thing in the jungle.

They then swung the rest of the way because they wanted to go home and play with their toys. They lived happily ever after.

Jessica Rebelo (7)
Westminster Cathedral RC Primary School, London

Daisy's Jungle Story

At some long, prickly vines Ellie and Spencer swung on the green, long vines. Ellie, Spencer the elf and Ellie's cuddly brown bear were having loads of fun. Ellie the brave, adventurous girl and the smart elf jumped on the dark, hard ground and met a scaly, slimy snake. The snake was ready to pounce.

Ellie the brave girl, the frightened bear and the smart elf were so scared their legs wanted to run away.

They were running and running until they bumped into a lion. The big furry lion said, 'Come over here.' Ellie the brave, adventurous girl and the clever elf hopped onto the golden lion's back and Ellie said it was nice and warm.

The lion stopped under some vines and Ellie and Spencer the elf got back to Ellie's cuddly warm house.

Daisy Riley (7)
Westminster Cathedral RC Primary School, London

Amy Leigh's Jungle Story

Ellie, Spencer and a silly little bear were delighted that Spencer had invited them to go to a big, deadly, scary and big jungle. They were swinging on vines.

They were walking slowly and were scared. All of a sudden a huge king cobra with a pattern running down its body appeared.

The snake pounced and stuck its slithery black tongue at them. Its poisonous pattern ran down its back.

Something was then rattling in the bushes like a baby's rattling toy. Ellie and Spencer were scared and so was the silly little bear.

'Do you want a ride?' said a lion to Ellie, Spencer and the silly little bear and they said yes.

Finally, they swung on humongous trees that led Ellie and Spencer back to Ellie's house with her loving family.

Amy Leigh Dunn (7)
Westminster Cathedral RC Primary School, London

Dylan's Jungle Story

Ellie and Spencer were in the damp, silent jungle but then they saw a giant baddy, the creature let out a loud hiss.

It was a venomous snake with a stripy pattern, it almost hypnotised Ellie!

They rushed past the python and it slithered after them but randomly a tree fell on the snake. The snake was executed.

The lion leapt in front of Ellie and fought off the python. The lion pounced back and helped them to get on his hairy back.

The lion dashed wildly, making the elf very cold as leaves scraped past him. The lion was so fast they fell off his back!

They came to some slippery vines and then approached home. They carefully climbed down and went back home.

Dylan Gething (6)

Westminster Cathedral RC Primary School, London

Harry's Jungle Story

Ellie and Spencer went to the jungle, there was a little bear on the vine. They said, 'We will call you Ted, not Ted, Mighty Ted!'

They bumped into a viper, it was hunting through the jungle. He looked like he was going to help them, but... it chased them to something furry.

It was a big predator so the snake was the prey and the snake slithered back home.

It was a lion, they were shocked. 'Argh! Help!' went Ted and Ellie.

The lion was friendly, he let them ride on him home. They liked the jungle, they were sad to leave.

They swung home and Spencer went to his tree house and had an elf party while Ellie joined in the party.

Harry Antony Hurley (7)

Westminster Cathedral RC Primary School, London

Akua's Jungle Story

One night Ellie was woken up by a tapping on her window, it was Spencer. They flew above the rooftops.

All of a sudden Ellie and Spencer met a devious snake who hypnotised Ellie, but he couldn't hypnotise Spencer.

Spencer quickly shook Ellie to keep her focused. Then Spencer told Ellie, 'Run!' The snake thought he could obviously catch them but he couldn't.

All of a sudden Ellie and Spencer met a gigantic lion. Ellie and Spencer were trembling in fear.

The lion didn't hurt them at all, he just led them home.

Finally, Ellie swung wildly on the vines all the way back home.

Akua Oppong (7)

Westminster Cathedral RC Primary School, London

Aaron's Jungle Story

Ellie was an adventurous girl, Spencer was a little elf and Bolt was the intelligent teddy. They swung on skinny green vines. They swung through the dark windy jungle.

There was a huge snake hissing like a rattle - *rat-a-tat-tat*. Bolt knew it was a cobra. They were scared like scared cats. 'Argh!'

They ran far, far away from the cobra and never went back to the cobra ever again.

They then saw a bright golden lion coming out from the green palm trees.

They were happy because he took them home and he was friendly.

They swung and sneaked in their home.

Aaron Jeriah Barclay (7)

Westminster Cathedral RC Primary School, London

Isabella's Jungle Story

One stormy night Ellie was woken by a tapping on her window. Ellie told Spencer the elf she wanted to go on a wild adventure.

They saw a slithery snake that looked scary.

The poisonous, dangerous snake said, 'If you don't go I will curl around you!' So they ran.

They paused for a minute to look at a lion then the lion said to Ellie and Spencer the elf, 'Do you want to play?'

They climbed on the lion's back and, *swoosh*, the lion took them home.

They lived happily ever after.

Isabella De Freitas (7)
Westminster Cathedral RC Primary School, London

Daniel's Jungle Story

A long time ago there were two people called Ellie and Spencer the elf, they were going into a damp jungle, everything was going fine until... there was a devious snake!

All of them were petrified and ran as fast as they could!

They ran as fast as they could and the snake was slithering up to them...

They suddenly found a nice lion. They didn't know it was nice.

The lion took them back home.

Ellie and Spencer lived happily ever after.

Daniel Germachew Mulugeta (7)

Westminster Cathedral RC Primary School, London

Frederick's Jungle Story

All of a sudden Ellie the brave person went out with Spencer and the teddy went swinging. They met a slithering snake. The snake said, 'Where are you going?' Then they ran away. They quickly ran before the snake hypnotised them.
They met a furry, kind lion. They were so shocked. The kind, furry lion offered them a ride.
They swung happily ever after.

Frederick Oloke (7)
Westminster Cathedral RC Primary School, London

Logan's Jungle Story

One stormy, dark night Ellie and Spencer swung like Tarzan through the bright green leaves. They flew across the rooftops like a bat.

They wanted to escape the jungle but a colourful, hungry snake was going to eat them alive.

They ran as fast as they could but with his slippery, slimy tail he chased them so they ran even faster than they were before!

They heard a bush rattling very quickly. It was a lion. He was big. They thought he was going to hurt them but actually he was nice. He was so scary he scared away the snake. He said, 'I will give you a ride home.'

Soon they were home in no time.

Logan Watts (7)
Westminster Cathedral RC Primary School, London

Tia's Jungle Story

Spencer and Ellie went to the jungle. They had lots of fun and they saw monkeys and lots of elephants. They also saw all sorts of animals. They then saw a big, long, scary snake. The snake got closer and closer until the snake tried to eat Spencer and Ellie.

They ran away but the snake caught them but then they got too fast.

Next Spencer and Ellie met a tiger. Spencer and Ellie said there was a snake catching them so the tiger helped them find their way home.

They then saw more animals on the way back home. Finally they went home and swung on some branches, they were really long.

Tia Williams (6)

Westminster Cathedral RC Primary School, London

125

Eva's Jungle Story

One night there was a big tap on Ellie's window, it was Spencer the elf. Spencer said, 'Do you want to go to the jungle?'
Ellie said, 'Yes.'
Ellie and Spencer flew to the jungle. When Ellie and Spencer got to the jungle Ellie and Spencer saw a snake. The snake tried to eat Ellie and Spencer so Ellie and Spencer ran as fast as they could to get away from the snake.
Next Ellie and Spencer met a gigantic lion. The lion was friendly and the orange lion showed them the way back home.
Ellie and Spencer swung back home.

Eva Ornelas (6)
Westminster Cathedral RC Primary School, London

Bettiel's Jungle Story

One night there was a boy called Spencer. He held Ellie's hand and they went out through the window. They both jumped out of the window. When they got to the jungle they saw a snake, the snake tried to catch both of them.

After that they saw a lion, they thought that it was not friendly but luckily the lion was friendly.

They both went on the lion's back and they went through the jungle.

They both swung back home, then Ellie slept. They both had a great adventure.

Bettiel Tech-Lu (6)

Westminster Cathedral RC Primary School, London

Samuel's Jungle Story

Ellie and Spencer went to the dark and green jungle at midnight. Ellie was sleepy. They swung from branches.

Suddenly, a snake appeared from the middle of nowhere. Ellie and Spencer were worried. They ran as fast as they could.

Suddenly, a friendly, yellow, smooth lion appeared from the shadow. They were frightened.

The lion gave them a ride back home.

Ellie said bye to Spencer and they lived happily ever after.

Samuel Emanuel (6)

Westminster Cathedral RC Primary School, London

Santiago's Jungle Story

Spencer woke Ellie up to go on an adventure. Ellie and Spencer swung on the green, beautiful branches.

Ellie and Spencer were really scared of the snake but Spencer was also really brave and scared the snake away from his best friend, Ellie. Ellie ran away from the green, scary snake.

The friendly lion was sad and Spencer and his best friend, Ellie, cheered the lion up so the lion let Spencer and Ellie on his back. Spencer and Ellie had a ride on the lion's back.

The lion showed Ellie and Spencer the way to her house so they rode on the green, beautiful branches and got home. Ellie went back to bed to sleep. Spencer went back to his house.

Santiago Silva Pereira (6)

Westminster Cathedral RC Primary School, London

Edward's Jungle Story

One day Ellie and Spencer the elf went to the jungle. They swung from tree to tree.

Ellie and Spencer the elf saw a long, long, long, long snake. They were scared as the snake was huge.

On their way, they saw a friendly lion. The lion told them to ride at his back and the lion took them around the jungle.

At night they swung back home. 'It was a fun day,' they said, 'and we had lots of fun.'

Edward Chahin (6)
Westminster Cathedral RC Primary School, London

Connie's Jungle Story

Once upon a time Ellie and Spencer went to the green jungle. Ellie and Spencer were swinging on green vines with a dark and light brown monkey. They saw a green and light brown snake.

After that they met a friendly, lonely lion. Ellie and Spencer then rode on the lion.

The lion dropped Ellie and Spencer back home to bed with Ellie's kitten and they lived happily ever after.

Connie Collins-Platt (6)

Westminster Cathedral RC Primary School, London

Iara's Space Story

Ellie and Spencer went to space. Then an alien appeared and saw Ellie and Spencer catching stars.

The alien took Ellie and Spencer away in a saucer. They flew through the sky and saw lots of stars. Then they saw a monster with a long tongue and three eyes.

Finally the alien took Ellie home in his saucer and they lived happily ever after.

Iara Machado Costa (6)

Westminster Cathedral RC Primary School, London

Sophia's Jungle Story

One night Ellie was sleeping, Ellie had a very good dream. There was a big tap on the window, it was Spencer the elf. Spencer said, 'Do you want to go on an adventure?' She flung out of the sheets and Ellie and Spencer arrived at some vines. They swung on the vines.

They landed very close to a snake, they were so scared that they ran away, but they didn't know where they were going. They weren't looking where they were going!

Ellie and Spencer bumped into a lion, they were a bit scared at first but they made friends. The friendly lion took them on an adventure, they had lots of fun but they were happier when they were back at home.

Sophia Soares (6)

Westminster Cathedral RC Primary School, London

Samira's Jungle Story

One nice, calm night Ellie the adventurous, brave girl and Spencer the quick, magical elf went swinging wildly through the vines. When they got to the jungle a fairy appeared so Ellie and Spencer said, 'Are you lost?'
'Yes, can you help us?'
'Of course, this way.' They took them and they went to the Queen of Happiness and she just appeared to them and so did the King of Sadness and they celebrated the celebration of their married kids with Ellie and Spencer and they lived happily ever after.

Samira Chaud (7)
Westminster Cathedral RC Primary School, London

The Storyboards

Here are the fun storyboards
children could choose from...

MAGICAL ADVENTURE

JUNGLE TALE

PIRATE ADVENTURE

SPACE STORY

ZOO ADVENTURE